Cornelia Funke

THE MONSTER FROM THE BLUE PLANET

Illustrated by Elys Dolan

Barrington Stoke

First published in 2015 in Great Britain by
Barrington Stoke Ltd
18 Walker Street, Edinburgh, EH3 7LP

www.barringtonstoke.co.uk

Title of the original German edition:
Leselöwen – Monstergeschichten
© 1993 Loewe Verlag GmbH, Bindlach

Illustrations © 2015 Elys Dolan
translation © 2015 barrington stoke

A CIP catalogue record for this book is available from the British Library upon request

ISBN: 978-1-78112-430-7

Printed in China by Leo

This book has dyslexia friendly features

CONTENTS

Chapter 1
A Small Blue Planet

Once upon a time, a girl called Zaleb lived on a planet called Balbaz. Zaleb loved nothing more than stories about faraway planets and all the strange monsters that lived there.

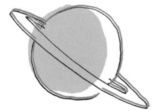

The story that Zaleb loved best of
all was about a little blue planet called
Earth. Strange monsters lived there.
They had no fur and only two eyes
and two arms each. Many years ago,
Zaleb's grandfather had travelled to that
strange planet. He had taken pictures
of the scary monsters and Zaleb had put
the pictures on the wall above her bed.

On Zaleb's birthday, one of her presents was a small spaceship. She decided to go to Earth and catch one of the monsters there to keep as a pet. All of her friends had at least one pet from another planet already.

Early that morning, Zaleb set off.

She left the silver hills of her home planet behind her and entered the endless night of the stars. She flew past scorching suns. She crossed blazing meteor showers. She dodged red-hot comets. At last she floated in the yellow light of the strange sun over the small blue planet.

Zaleb switched on her M.Y.I.S. – her Make Yourself Invisible System – as she dropped down to Earth. She had hoped to find a lovely green meadow like the ones in her grandfather's pictures.

She wanted to see a meadow where little flowers grew on the ground and big flowers grew on wooden trunks that reached up to the sky. She wanted to see the Earth monsters run and play in the flowers.

But all Zaleb could find were huge blocks of grey stone and long grey snakes with smelly metal beetles crawling all over them.

It was only as the strange sun was about to set that Zaleb spotted what she was looking for – a green meadow filled with white flowers. And in the middle of it there was an Earth monster!

This Earth monster was as pale and
bare as the ones in the pictures that
Zaleb's grandfather had brought home,
and it really did only have two eyes
and two thin arms like sticks. Its eyes

had an odd wet shimmer about them
and there was a huge ugly bump in the
middle of its face. But it wasn't as scary
as Zaleb had imagined. In fact, she was
a little bit disappointed.

The Earth monster stood up on its hind legs and moved its jaw in a very odd way, as it shoved things into its little round mouth. On its head there was some straggly yellow hair, which almost fell into its eyes. Its body was covered in weird clothes of many colours. Zaleb thought they looked rather silly.

Zaleb floated her spaceship down as gently as she could. She hovered right above the head of the Earth monster and switched on the trapping beam. The pale little Earth monster disappeared from the meadow as if it had never been there.

CHAPTER 2

THE EARTH MONSTER

In the blink of an eye, Zaleb's spaceship was many sun systems away from Earth. Zaleb was on her way home to the planet of Balbaz. Her new pet was on board.

The monster made a terrible noise as Zaleb used the trapping beam to put it in a cage. It jumped up and down like a wild thing. It rattled the bars of the cage with its little claws and it let out awful shouts and yelps. The noise reminded Zaleb of the snorts of moon pigs and the screams of crystal monkeys.

Zaleb put on her translation helmet and stepped up to the cage. Then she jumped back with fright.

"You ugly monster!" the little beast shouted into Zaleb's face. "Let me out right now!"

Zaleb couldn't believe her ears. "Did you say 'monster'?" she yelled. "You're the monster – not me! And from now on you are my pet!"

"What?" the pale Earth monster hissed.

It rattled the bars of the cage with such fury that Zaleb stepped further back again. Even with her translation helmet on, she could not make sense of the angry words the little monster was saying.

All of a sudden, the little monster huddled down at the bottom of the cage and started to sob.

Silver drops of water ran from its eyes and down its pale face. Zaleb was shocked. Was it ill? Did it have travel sickness?

"I want to go home!" the monster sobbed. "I want to go back home."

"What do you mean, 'go back home'?" Zaleb asked in surprise. "Monsters don't have homes."

"You're the monster, not me!" The pale creature sniffed. "My name is Izzy and of course I have a home!"

"Well, I have a home too!" Zaleb said. She was very angry now. "My home is the planet Balbaz. It has silver mountains and multi-coloured seas that shimmer like glass. It has seven moons, and each of them is a different colour. And the gravity on each moon is different too."

The little Earth monster stopped sobbing and it looked at Zaleb in wonder.

"Seven moons?" it asked. "Is that true? We only have one moon, you see."

"Yes, of course it's true," Zaleb said. And all of a sudden, the eyes of the Earth monster shone like two little stars.

"I would love to see those moons," the little monster said. "But I will not be your pet."

Zaleb looked at the little Earth monster for a moment before she spoke. 'My friends will laugh at me,' she thought. But then she pressed a button and the cage disappeared.

"Come on then," Zaleb said, and she gave the little Earth monster a shy smile. "Come with me, Izzy. I will show you the seven moons of my planet. You can be my visitor for a while, and then I will take you home."

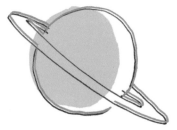

CHAPTER 3

THE WISHING MOON

Izzy stayed on Zaleb's planet for three months, while only three hours passed at home. She saw the silver mountains, and the multi-coloured seas, and the seven moons.

"The purple moon is the wishing moon," Zaleb told Izzy. "Do you have a crazy crazy wish that nothing else in the world can make come true?"

"I do," Izzy said.

"Well, then," Zaleb told her. "Write your wish on a piece of paper and put it outside the window. If you're lucky, the north wind will blow it all the way to the wishing moon."

And so, one starlit night when the wishing moon shone full, Izzy did as Zaleb told her.

In the middle of the night, Izzy heard a knock on the window.

"How odd," she said to herself. "Zaleb's house is on the 5th floor! How can anyone be knocking at the window?"

Izzy opened the curtains and saw an eye as big as a car tyre. The eye looked back at her from outside the window.

Izzy's hands shook as she opened the window and a shimmering silver claw came in. Izzy saw a little piece of paper pierced on the smallest nail of the claw.

"Is this yours?" asked a voice that was as deep as a well.

Izzy read her own spidery writing on the paper. It said, "I wish I could fly through the night on the back of a dragon."

Izzy looked into the big round eye and nodded.

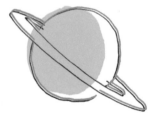

"Well, come on then!" the deep voice said.

And then the massive claw turned towards Izzy so that she could climb on. The claw lifted her out into the moonlit night and up onto a huge scaly back, which blocked out the stars like a mountain. There were two great wings that stood up like sails, one on the left and one on the right.

"Are you sitting comfortably?" the dragon asked. It turned its neck so it could see Izzy.

"Yes," Izzy whispered. She could hear her heartbeat, as loud as a drum.

The dragon opened its wings, and it flew up into the night sky.

They flew higher and higher, until the moons and the stars seemed closer than the lights of the planet below them. Izzy's hair fluttered in the ice-cold wind, but she snuggled close to the dragon's body and that kept her warm.

On they flew while the seven moons moved across the sky.

At last Izzy noticed that the dragon's wings were slowing down and that they were going lower and lower, closer and closer to the city below.

"What are you doing?" she shouted.

"The sun is about to rise!" the dragon shouted back. "I can feel it. I need to take you home."

"Oh," Izzy said. She felt a tear run down her nose, but she wiped it off so the dragon didn't see it.

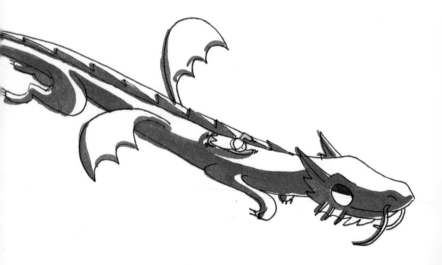

"What will happen if I throw another piece of paper into the north wind?" Izzy asked, as the dragon put her back into the spare bedroom of Zaleb's house.

"A wish of this kind will be granted only once," the dragon said. "Farewell, my friend."

And then it was gone.

Izzy heard the swoosh of wings as the dragon flew off into the night. She saw a black shadow go past the purple wishing moon as it set.

Every night until she left Balbaz, Izzy looked out the window of Zaleb's house on the 5th floor, but the wishing moon dragon never came back.

CHAPTER 4

A MIDNIGHT SNACK

A few nights after the dragon's visit, Izzy woke up with a jump.

She was very thirsty. She stumbled and rubbed her eyes as she felt her way into the dark kitchen of Zaleb's house.

Izzy opened the fridge – and froze.

"Will you shut that door!" a horrible voice said. "Get a move on!"

There was a monster! It was on the middle shelf of the fridge, between a plate of sausages and a bowl of jelly.

It was a disgusting yellow monster with green spots and a wide mouth full of teeth as sharp as needles. It held a sausage in one claw, and in the other it held a cucumber.

The monster grunted and burped. "Stop gawping at me," it said. "You've stared at me long enough. Shut the door. Chop, chop!"

Izzy couldn't move. She stood there as if she was frozen to the ground, and she stared at the monster as it chomped away on its midnight snack.

The monster giggled. "What's up, goggle eyes? Have you never seen a fridge monster before?" It put its scaly arm into the jelly and licked its fingers with delight. "Yummy yum yum yum," it said. "I do like it here. But I've had enough of you!"

Splat! The monster threw a dollop of jelly in Izzy's face and then it pulled the fridge door shut from the inside.

Izzy turned around and tip-toed into Zaleb's bedroom.

"There's a big yellow monster in the fridge," she told her. "It's eating jelly and sausages."

"Go back to bed," Zaleb mumbled. "It was just a bad dream."

And then Zaleb turned over and started to snore.

Izzy shrugged and went back into the kitchen. From the outside, the fridge looked perfectly normal. Izzy opened the door again.

"You again!" the monster snarled. "Go back to your bed, shorty!"

The monster was now on the next shelf down. Its face was covered with what was left of a box of 10 eggs. The jelly bowl looked like it had been washed clean. The tub that had held the sausages had nothing left in it.

"Don't you have any cheese?" the monster growled. It scratched its belly with egg yolk fingers and grunted.

Izzy shook her head.

"No? Well, I'll just have to find a better fridge then, won't I?" the monster said.

With that, the monster jumped down and landed in front of Izzy. It looked up at her with squinty yellow eyes like a cat's.

"See you later, shorty!" the monster bellowed. "Cheers!" It pushed past Izzy and wiped its 14 sticky fingers on her pyjamas on the way.

The monster crossed the kitchen with a few clumsy hops, pulled itself up onto the window sill, opened the window and jumped out into the darkness.

Izzy ran over to the window and looked out. There was nothing. Only the full scarlet moon in the dark sky. So Izzy closed the empty fridge and crawled

back into bed. She was still thirsty. She hadn't even got herself a drink in the end. Never mind. She really didn't feel like going back to the fridge now.

"Did you sleep well?" Zaleb's mother asked Izzy in the morning.

"No, I didn't sleep very well at all," Izzy said. "I will be sorry to leave Balbaz, but I think I may sleep better at home!"

"Perhaps you would like to come and visit again?" Zaleb's mother said.

"Please do," Zaleb begged. "Come and stay again, my friend from the Blue Planet!"

And that's just what Izzy did. But that's another story ...

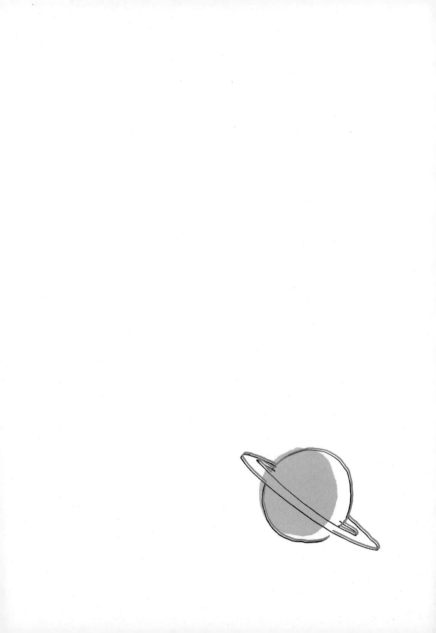

Our books are tested
for children and young people by
children and young people.

Thanks to everyone who consulted on
a manuscript for their time and effort in
helping us to make our books better
for our readers.

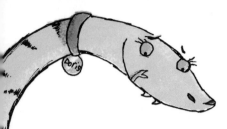

Have you read
all the
Little Gems ?

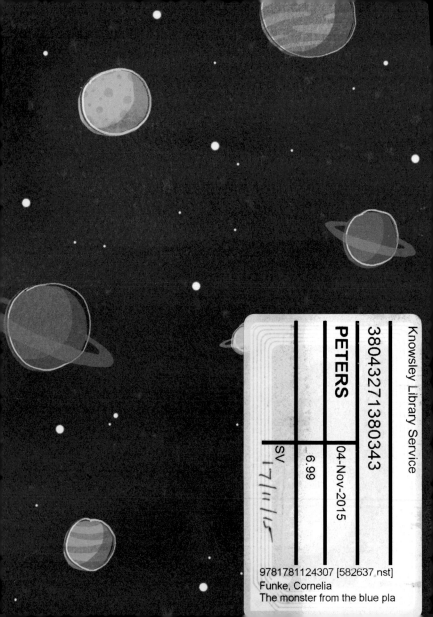